DORA

by

Dennis Otu

ISBN 978 - 31053 - 4 - 5

First Printing, May, 1995
second edition, 2014

first edition by
Ginao-Chris (Nig.) Company, 2 Metsarun Street,
Off Okere Ugborikoko Road,
Okumagba Layout, Warri.

Second edition
BookBuilders• Editions Africa
2 Awosika, Bodija Estate
Ibadan, Nigeria
mobile: 0809 920 9106
cover: Omnicraft, Ibadan

ALSO BY THE AUTHOR
Quotes of Who's Who
Love Made Easy

The characters in this book are imaginary.
No reference is intended to any person; living of dead.
Some of the names of places mentioned
in this book are real.

Endorsements

A very good attempt. Good for young readers. Teaches a lot of morals and the virtues of self determination and also destiny. Recommended as literature text for JSS I.

> **- R.O. Aziza (Mrs.)**
> **Dept. of Nigerian Languages, College of Education, Warri**

This book is a delightful compendium of the activities that made Nigeria recognizable and Nigerians a dictionary of unique sensibilities.

> **-Adetokunbo Abiola**
> **The Observer**

DORA is a short, racy and tightly woven story that x-rays the decadent culture of an emergent modern Nigerian society.

> **- Eni-Jones Umuko**
> **DELSU, Abraka**

Our people are enterprising, hard-working people, but every opportunity for legitimate business has been blocked by the army, their wives and their families'.

> **- Chief M.K.O. Abiola**

DEDICATION

Dedicated to my mother,
Madam C. T. Dafe on her 50th birthday
(April 13, 1945 – April 13, 1995).

Compatriots arise and let us build
one virile nation for the sake of
our children for their tomorrow,
I give my today to write DORA.

The love I have for my fatherland,
inspired me to write this book so
that there could be a better place
for our children and children's children.
May God bless our nation.

Dennis Ogheneare Otu
"OTU DEN"
1995

FOREWORD

It is not often that one confronts the possibility of a new genre in literature. What one finds is a mere repetition of existing literary possibilities or a nebulous arrangement of literary values or practice. Dennis Otu's new novel, *Dora*, thankfully does not fall within the parameters of this disturbing tradition. It is an attempt to transcend an already existing prerogative. It is also an angry and sometimes bewildered assessment of the socio-political arrangement of this nation. Of course, mention must be made of the fact that it is a morality tale, a criticism against evil, and thumbs-up for good. Furthermore, this book is a delightful compendium of activities that make Nigeria recognizable and Nigerians a dictionary of unique sensibilities.

First, let us discuss Dora's attempt to transcend the old order. The author, undeniably, writes a romance story, a tale of love, a compelling *tour de force* of Dora's love life. It is, of course, successful. We are engaged with Dora and her best friend's love travails and successes. We are enthralled that Dora's love experiment, true to the romantic tradition of a poor girl marrying a rich man, was crowned with success. In a rare sense in African fiction, Dennis Otu merges this plethora of romantic activities within the ambiance of social criticism. He seems to be saying "look, you can fall in love, you can be romantic, but you are living in Nigeria where things do not work."

Dennis Otu has merged social criticism with romance - he is one of first writers to journey through this possibility.

Needless to say, Dora is a morality tale. Apart from the perpetrator of the murder of Dora's senior brother all the crooks and bad guys were caught, and they were forced to face the long arm of the law. The prostitute who flirts around and could not get married. The young men who rob in order to acquire immense wealth and prestige. The robbers who waylay pedestrians and strip them of their valuables and hard earned money. Dennis Otu juxtaposed their travails with the idyllic love life of Dora, and the morality and sanity with which Dora's husband acquired his wealth, he seems to be setting them up as examples to be emulated, as a combination that would serve as a pancreas to the present distortion inherent in this nation's social fabric.

But the strength of this book does not lie in this alone. Its chronological presentation of the social realities prevalent in this country gives it a verisimilitude that is recognizable and familiar. You witness the power surge that Nigerians experience. There is the corruption that has become a disease in our social setting. There is the harrowing spectre that occurs on a daily basis on Nigerian roads. You see the sexual irresponsibility that has destroyed the moral fabric of this nation. There is no doubt about it, this book is not only a romance but a criticism of our values. Through it, you can see the skeletal structure underneath the fleshy coverings of our foibles, mistakes, saddening corruption and undeniable weaknesses.

Of course, there should be more drama, more integration of these acerbic criticisms within a dramatic framework, there should be a more confident rendition of experimental matter, but the sure handling of syntax and sentences recommends that this should be a book to be appreciated.

Adetokunbo Abiola
Art Editor, The Observer
Benin City.

ACKNOWLEDGMENT

I sincerely wish to express my profound gratitude to the following and others too numerous to mention whose support in one way or the other led to the birth of this book.

- Mr. Eni-Jones Umuko - the author of PRINCESS ESILOKUN;
- Mrs. R. O. Aziza of the Department of Nigerian Languages, College of Education, Warri;
- Mr. Daley Udoewa,
- Mr. Francis Onochie of the Delta Broadcasting Service, Warri;
- Mr. Adetokunbo Abiola of *The Observer* Newspapers, Benin City and
- Mr. Jeyere D. Ugbeye of Delta Broadcasting Service, Warri.

I thank you all for going through this book and offering useful suggestions.

I am also indebted to Prince Joseph Onofurho, Mr. Francis Ovie Ovire, Mr. Matthew Enamutor, Mr. Lola Falobi, Okenze S.I. Obinna, Mr. M.O. Urhobotie and Ekeh L. Chinedu. Special thanks to Miss Mercy Solomon.

I am grateful to Mrs. Florence Emadifie, Mr. & Mrs. Emanerame, Mrs. Patience Ihimekpen, Mrs. Bibian Enebeli, Mrs. Silver Unukarekpe, Mr. Williams Onoriode and Mrs. Margaret Okpako.

I am deeply grateful to those who stood by me during the making of my other book: *Love Made Easy*.

One

It was night in Urhuoka and within an hour NEPA had plunged the whole town into darkness four times. Urhuoka is a busy commercial town along the highway that leads to the Eastern State. Urhuoka is close to the University town of Abraka. At the road junction that links Urhuoka to the highway is a house painted green. This house belongs to Mr. Woba Zome, a retired prison staff. Mr. Zome's street known as Wandia is a very busy one especially in the early hours of the day.

Beside Zome's house is a bungalow belonging to a wealthy trader, Kuma. Mr. Kuma who has a pretty wife and a daughter called Ngozi, is well known in the town.

Zome and Kuma were playing a second set of draughts when NEPA struck for the fifth time. Both men shifted their attention from the draughts they were playing as a result of the darkness, and deliberated on the issue of erratic power supply by NEPA.

"NEPA has always been a big problem in this town, in fact, the whole country," Zome said.

"Oh don't mind them and at the end of the month they send huge bills for settlement without rendering any service. They have destroyed all my electronics," Kuma added as the discussion progressed.

"You see Kuma, my son Joe wrote to me that he had never witnessed blackout since his arrival in the United States of America over five years ago."

"Just imagine that! Here they take the light every second, and that reminds me, how is Joe after all?"

"Joe is doing fine. He phoned about two months ago."

"I remember vividly," Kuma stated.

As both men discussed more national issues especially the recent national strike and the fuel pump price increase and how it affects the downtrodden masses, NEPA restored the electricity and in unison children and even grown-ups shouted, "eh light don come, dem don bring light."

But as Zome and Kuma were about to resume the game, the light went off again. Out of frustration they packed up the game and went to their respective homes to sleep for the night.

The families of Zome and that of Kuma were unique as Zome and Kuma have been friends for a long time. Kuma was godfather to Joe, Zome's son.

The friendship of both families was rekindled when upon retirement from the prison service, Zome came home to settle down and enjoy his retirement with his kinsmen.

The same evening when Zome and Kuma were playing draughts the plane Joe boarded from America landed at the Murtala Muhammed International Airport, Ikeja, Lagos at about 7 p.m. Joe enjoyed the ten-hour flight from America as he was treated to classical music throughout the journey.

The airport was very busy that evening as wives and relations of ECOMOG soldiers sent to Liberia were around to bid farewell to their husbands and brothers who were recently drafted to the war-torn country to keep the peace.

Joe had planned to come home in three months time, but two days ago he received an urgent call from a business partner in Lagos, who urged him to take the next available flight to Lagos. The tone of the message was very urgent so he decided to breeze in but made up his mind not to go down to Urhuoka to see his father and sister, Dora.

At the arrival hall of the airport, three men, richly dressed welcomed Joe to Nigeria. He recognized only one of them known as "Coach".

"The boss has been expecting you," Coach said to Joe as they shook hands.

" . . . I know and that is why I'm here. How is he?" Joe asked.

"He is fine and you shall soon meet him." Coach said to Joe.

Coach had met Joe at a party in America some years ago. He talked Joe into some business deals and right from that time Joe became Badmiller's business partner in America. Coach introduced himself to Joe as personal assistant to Badmiller.

Joe entered a white Concord Benz car belonging to Badmiller and he was driven to Badmiller's house. Joe had been dealing with Badmiller for the past two years and he had always felt that Badmiller, who is the King of the "Black Gold" empire could be dangerous.

They had done a lot of business together in the past two years and presently they were involved in a deal worth half a billion dollars with an oil marketing consortium known as Five Stars Oil.

Badmiller who was about fifty years old had made up his mind to do away with Joe immediately he signed the contract agreement, because he felt that Joe would one day rise up against him as some of his partners had done in the past.

Badmiller lived in an isolated location far away from the airport, after a long drive Joe and the three men arrived at Badmiller's place where he met him at the swimming pool with a white lady. The compound was huge with massive steel gates.

Immediately Joe arrived, Badmiller dismissed the white lady who later retired to bed in one of the fifty-bedrooms in the palatial house. The lady has been married to Badmiller for ten years without any issue.

Joe was warmly received by Badmiller and when they finally completed the contract deal, which was the shipment of crude oil from Nigeria to Five Stars Oil in America, both men including Coach sat down for a drink and food. It was almost twelve midnight.

At a point, Joe and Badmiller took a little walk and started discussing business, leaving Coach and others behind. Before Joe and Badmiller returned, the three men who brought Joe from the airport had carried out the instruction of their boss by dropping a poisonous substance into Joe's glass which he filled to the brim before they took a walk. Joe gulped some of the drink when they returned and he started felling dizzy; after some moments Joe dropped dead.

*   *   *

It was a chilly harmattan morning and all of a sudden Zome sprang out of a frightful sleep. He sat at the edge of the bed and started recalling the terrible dream he had about his son, Joe, throughout the night. As he was recalling the dream bit by bit, he heard voices outside and he opened his door and saw a large crowd around a Mercedes Benz car neatly packed in front of his house. The time was just six in the morning. Zome could not understand the cause of   the   uproar until he moved forward to see things for himself.

This car was not here before we went to bed last night, Zome said to himself as he moved closer to the car. On approaching he discovered that the only occupant in the car was his eldest son, Joe. He was wearing a long sleeved shirt, black tie with an ash-coloured shoe and a golden wrist-watch. His briefcase was by his side.

As Zome drew close to the car, he observed that Joe was as cold as a frozen fish. He was stone dead.

Zome who was almost collapsing was led back to the house by Kuma and some elderly persons attracted to the scene. He was surrounded inside the house by sympathizers and at that time too, Dora was being consoled by her friend, Ngozi and some other girls in the neighbourhood.

"This is very strange in the history of Urhuoka," a bewildered sympathizer said to a friend.

"So many strange things happen these days," the friend replied as they took the last glance at the body of Joe inside the car before they joined other sympathizers in the house.

"We must do something fast as we cannot afford to leave the body like that in the car," said Kuma to other men.

"I'm confused, but where do we really start from?" Someone asked.

"This matter must be reported to the police immediately," Kuma stated. Kuma and two others immediately left for the police station where the matter was reported and before long a team of policemen stormed Zome's compound. The police investigation was fruitless as there was no clue to lead them to arrest anyone around.

The briefcase that was found in the car by policemen drafted to the scene contained fifty thousand American dollars and an international passport, and other documents belonging to the late Joe Zome.

The passport stamp revealed that Joe, who had been in the United States for the past five years, left

America the previous day. That was all the information the police could get at.

An autopsy carried out later by the police doctor showed that Joe died as a result of an overdose of a poisonous substance. According to the doctor's report, Joe died within minutes of the poison hitting him.

Zome wondered who the hell could have done that to his son. *Who poisoned Joe, my son and for what motive?* This thought ran through his mind but he could not find any answer.

He was never himself after that day. He had to bury his own son whom he sponsored to America from the gratuity he received from the prisons' service, which he joined as a recruit. It was during the colonial period that Zome was enlisted into the prisons' service. He rose through the ranks to become an assistant superintendent of prisons before he retired.

The thought of Joe's mysterious death hastened Zome to his own grave. He had spoken to Joe on the telephone about two months before he died and from the discussion Joe never indicated that he was coming home.

Two

From the telephone conversation, Zome had with his late son it was concluded that Dora who had just received her SSS III result with good grades, would join him in the United States to study mass communication. It was agreed that he would send enough money to take care of Dora's travelling expenses and additional money for their father.

Joe also told his father that he should expect a Mercedes Benz for his personal use. At his retirement, Zome had a Volkswagen beetle but ten months after his retirement, he had an accident and his wife, Mariam, died on the spot, while himself and their daughter Dora, who was ten years old, were rushed to a nearby hospital and treated for severe injuries. As for the car it was a write-off.

It was a year after Zome got his gratuity and other entitlements that Joe travelled to America for a better future, since he was unable to secure a job in his own country having studied criminology in one of the universities.

*   *   *

Throughout the span of a man's life, so many things could happen, thought Zome to himself as he drank the last drop of the brandy from the glass.

Since the death of Joe, he drank continually and was virtually drunk from morning to night. He also took up smoking. His doctor had cautioned him that his habits were not good for his health, as his blood pressure kept rising. He had not seen his other children from his second wife since their marriage broke up.

When Zome was married to both wives, that is, before the fatal accident in which Mariam died, they were never at peace with each other for one day, until Clara, the second wife, left the marriage. Clara was the mother of the girl that was born after Joe, before Dora was born.

Zome got to know Clara when he was working at Kojoba Prison. They got married and had a girl, Charity and two boys, Paul and Crowder. It was while he was on transfer to another prison that the marriage broke up, and Clara who hailed from Onitsha left with her children.

Exactly ten months after Joe's death, Zome became very ill and was rushed to the only government hospital in Urhuoka, where he died two months later in the hospital.

The night before he joined his ancestors, Zome had told Dora to take life as she saw it.

"Dora, my daughter, you must be a good girl, considering that I was unable to send you to the University. It had been our plan to send you to America so you could further your studies, but the plan died with Joe, and ever since his death . . . I have never been the same again . . . you have to accept whatever happens to me."

". . . Oh father," Dora cut him short, "the doctor said you should rest and not talk too much."

"No, my daughter, let me talk for I might not have the chance and the strength again to talk with you in this manner," said the sick man.

"It is like you are the only one I have left in this world; I do not know the whereabouts of your other sister and brothers, but I pray that one day you people shall find each other and live together as brothers and sisters."

Immediately he had finished talking, the doctor came in with a nurse to give him the last injection and drugs for the day, and Dora was advised to let her father sleep.

$$\sim\!\sim\!\sim\!\sim\!\sim\!\sim\!\sim\!\sim\!\sim\!\sim\!\sim\!\sim\!\sim$$

Three

At six in the morning, Dora woke up from the floor in the hospital where she had laid throughout the night.

Her father was still sleeping when she left the hospital with some of his clothes that needed to be washed. When she returned at noon with her childhood friend, Ngozi they met the old man having his first meal of the day, baked beans and pap. The male ward of the hospital was crowded with people that afternoon because it was visiting time.

The two girls greeted Zome and took their seats on the available benches.

Dora added the rice she had prepared from home to the baked beans, but the old man took a little of this, he was satisfied with his meal.

Five minutes after the meal, a female nurse who had been attending to over one hundred and fifty patients in the ward came to Zome's bedside and gave him his drugs; which he took immediately.

The nurse beaming with smiles, told Dora that her father would be discharged the next day, which was Monday. When the doctor came in to check Zome some minutes after the nurse had left, he further confirmed this to Dora who was filled with joy, and Ngozi also shared the joyful news with her friend.

When it was time for Ngozi to go home, she opened her bag and brought out a card which read thus, "I wish you a speedy recovery". This she placed by Zome's bedside. He was glad at this and thanked the eighteen-year old girl, who was born the same year with Dora.

When Dora was seeing off her friend, she told her father that she was going to raise the five thousand naira they needed before he could be discharged. Aware that there was no way Dora could raise the money, Zome advised her to sell some of the expensive wrappers in his trunk.

That afternoon, Dora and Ngozi went to a money lender who bought four pieces of the wrappers for three thousand, five hundred naira.

"Ngozi, you have been very helpful to me since my father took ill. It's only God that can reward you for everything," Dora had said to Ngozi on their way from the money lender.

"But you don't have to talk that way Dora, after all why are we friends. Your problem is also mine."

Later that day, before Dora returned to the hospital, Ngozi took   one thousand naira from the money her parents had given to her to go back to school with and gave it to Dora.

Dora, who was already confused as to how to raise the balance was short of words of appreciation for her good friend, Ngozi.

"Thank you very much my only friend. You've proved to b e a real friend indeed. When my brother Joe died a lot of money was found in his briefcase. The police took everything to the station along with the car where his body was found. Nothing came out of the police investigation and the money and the car also disappeared. All efforts made by my father to get the money and the car back yielded no result. Until he took ill. I know that all this no doubt contributed to his illness, but I'm glad that he's leaving the hospital tomorrow."

When Ngozi noticed the tears flowing freely from Dora's eyes she quickly comforted her. When Ngozi was quite sure that Dora was herself again, they parted. While Dora was going back to the hospital having taken the last five hundred naira they had at home to complete the money, Ngozi headed for home.

That evening Kuma, who was away on a business trip when Zome was admitted, returned and Ngozi briefed him about everything and without waiting another moment he went to the hospital.

Four

The hospital was in pitch darkness when Dora got there. She was informed by her father that the electricity went off about five minutes before she got there.

Without wasting time, Dora went to a nearby store outside the hospital gate to get a stick of candle, which she lit by her father's bedside, just like others in the ward had done.

Dora narrated how she was able to sell the wrappers and how Ngozi had assisted her. She also told him that Ngozi won't be able to see him as she would be busy preparing to return to Enugu, where she was schooling.

Ngozi on her part had felt so bad that she could not wait for her friend's father to be discharged before leaving for school.

Dora had just finished narrating everything to her sick father, when Kuma walked into the male ward of the hospital accompanied by a nurse who brought him to Zome's bedside. Dora greeted him at once and left the two men.

"Oh, Kuma you are here, glad to see you," Zome said as he got out of the bed.

"I was surprised when my daughter Ngozi told me about   your condition, but I'm glad that you will be discharged tomorrow."

"That was what the doctor said," Zome said. "And Kuma I'm short of words to thank you and your entire family for everything. That your Ngozi is a sensible girl."

"Please, Zome do not go all that far, just relax yourself and Dora should get those wrappers back from whoever bought them and his money given back to him."

At that moment he brought out an envelope containing the sum of seven thousand naira and handed it over to Zome. "Take this for the hospital bill and any other expenses you may incur, but I must be on my way now."

Zome and Dora thanked Kuma for the money. They were flabbergasted.

"I keep on saying it, Kuma that you are more than a friend. You have been so helpful. Thank you very much may the Almighty God reward you."

"Oh that is alright, Zome see you tomorrow", Kuma said as he took leave of father and daughter.

When he had gone, Zome instructed Dora to return the money and get the wrappers from the money lender the following morning.

In Urhuoka where they lived, the roads were so bad that motorists found it extremely difficult to ply them. It was the transportation problem experienced by the people of Urhuoka, especially in the early hours of the day, that made Ngozi reason that she wouldn't be able to make it to the hospital and back home before taking off for school. The doctors might not discharge the sick man very early in the morning.

Politicians with their sugar-coated tongues had in the past promised the people of Urhuoka that they would tar their roads once they were voted into power, but they always reneged on these promises after scoring political victories.

With time the people became wiser and they have since vowed never to listen again when the politicians are preaching, because the more they listened to politicians the more they became hungry, the more they lived in darkness, the more their children stayed out of school, the more they did not have potable water to drink, the more there were no jobs for their children and the more their hospitals turned into mere consulting clinics.

It took the people of Urhuoka a long time to experience electricity and since they got National Electric Power Authority in the area, they have not known peace. If there were problems with their transformer, they were made to solve such problems. They would remain in darkness for as long as it took them to raise the money in order for NEPA to carry out the necessary repairs.

As for the electricity supply which was cut five minutes before Dora arrived at the hospital, it took another five days before the light was restored. For five days a government hospital was plunged into darkness because the hospital's stand-by generating plant had long been abandoned as a result of minor faults.

Relations of people in critical conditions at the hospital moved them to private clinics where twenty-four hour electricity supply was no problem, as they had faultless generating plants. Corpses in the mortuary were buried hastily to avoid decomposition.

Politicians also   capitalized on the problems of NEPA to promise the people constant electricity supply, but they soon forgot that this problem ever existed once they were voted into power. Politicians had in the past also promised to build bridges for the people, even where there was no river. The people had since learnt how to take their destiny in their own hands. They resolved never to wait for their leaders; civilians or soldiers, to do anything for them.

Five

At about midnight, just a few hours left for him to be discharged from the hospital, Zome gave up the ghost.

He took his last breath as the candle lit by his bedside burnt itself out in a pool of wax. It was a grave moment for Dora who cried her eyes out. As she wailed for her father, she was surrounded by the nurses on night duty. The senior among the nurses soon certified that Zome had died. He was immediately covered with a white bed sheet.

When the doctor who was to discharge him that morning heard of the sad news, he felt as bad as Dora felt, although he never cried, but his eyes were as red as flames of fire.

The news of the death spread far and wide, like fire in the harmattan season. Soon the death became the topic of discussion throughout Urhuoka and beyond.   Three days later, family members and friends including Kuma took the corpse home for a befitting burial.

Ngozi heard of the news at school and rushed home to stay with her friend throughout the seven days of the burial, but Dora refused to be comforted. On the day of the interment she had wished to be buried along with her father. She was advised to take heart and brace up to face the future boldly.

Life to Dora after the death of her father became one frustrating thing after another. Her father had died when she had least expected it and this made it more painful.

Six

As a girl who lost her mother when she was ten years old and eighteen when her father died, Dora decided to work hard to overcome this tragic misfortune. She started to trade, and at the same time she attended evening classes, believing that one day she would acquire the university education which the death of her brother and poverty robbed her of. To her the only key to success was education and no amount of wealth one acquired without higher education is good enough.

Kuma was impressed with how Dora did things on her own without support from anybody. One day he called her and gave her some money to boost her business.

Dora was so elated and in no time she became a successful trader in Urhuoka. She was never worried about how she was going to pay her education because she was full of hope that she would earn enough money to pay for her university fees. The future looked bright. The solution to her problem was just a matter of time.

One night, she thought seriously about her mother, father and brother, ". . . my father could not afford to send me to the university because we were poor and my brother Joe, who was the breadwinner and who was living in America died in mysterious circumstances." At the thought of this, she began to cry.

Dora also recalled how the Mercedes Benz in which Joe's corpse was found had vanished from the police station, along with all the money in the briefcase. There was no doubt that the money in the briefcase belonged to Joe.

All efforts made by her father before he died to retrieve the car, the money and get to the root of the cause of Joe's death yielded no fruit, as he was always asked to "come tomorrow" at the police station.

At a point, Dora's father became fed up with the whole process and regretted that the matter was reported to the police. He wished he had kept the money and the expensive car and buried his son without any report to the police. But as a man who decided to follow the legal process as was done in civilized places of the world, he soon learned that the society in which he belonged to was a lawless one. Until his death he swore never to trust the police. He was a good petitioner while he was a prison officer. He wrote several petitions to the Inspector-General of Police to protest the slipshod manner in which the police handled his son's death and the theft of the car and money but nothing positive came out of it.

Dora indicted the police for contributing to the death of her father. She felt that if the police had not confiscated the car and the money, her father would not have sunk into a deep depression which lead to his death and he would have been able to afford her university education.

Education to Dora was an asset which should not be taken away from a child. She never liked the police for one day and hated those in the corridors of power who oppress the people all the time.

She was also against a system where the rich got richer and the poor got poorer. To her, the rich ones in the society should emulate the few like Kuma and help to educate children from poor homes. She reasoned that once this was done, there would be no trace of illiteracy in the society and the development of the entire country would be rapid. She was always disappointed when this was not done, instead she saw pain and suffering on the faces of the people while the bourgeoisie were always smiling all the time with their children sent abroad for good education.

Her vexation with the society was to continue the following day when she heard on the radio that a police corporal had shot dead a bus driver who refused to part with ten naira. Dora felt bad throughout that day, because she saw no reason why the police that was meant to maintain law and order should turn around and start killing the citizens.

"... We've had enough of police brutality," she said to herself over and over again.

Dora wondered why the police that were being maintained by the tax payers' money   should be the peoples' killer. She felt that money should be allocated to projects that would benefit the masses instead of the police.

At the thought that there was nothing she could do to change things for the better, she became more annoyed and throughout that day she buried herself in deep thoughts.

"One day my tomorrow will come and I shall write about our societal madness."

Having said that, Dora decided to wait for her tomorrow that would come when it would come.

Seven

Ngozi having completed her university education and the compulsory one year National Youth Service Corps scheme, got a job teaching in a private secondary school, in Urhuoka, a job that she enjoyed doing, although it was very tasking.

But she had the misfortune of falling in love with Mike, a die-hard armed robber. This was unknown to her until things started unfolding.

Ngozi was not always happy despite the fact that she had a good job with an attractive salary. The man whom she thought loved her as she loved him was not always around her when she needed him. He always showered her with gifts and money, but a woman needed more than that. Every woman needs a man she can call her own. A man who cares and understands. A man to share her lonely moments with.

But Mike was not such a man. He was too busy robbing and killing people to think of women and children. He did not even know the whereabouts of the four children he had already. And this never bothered him.

Ngozi got to know Mike when she was a final year student in the university. One day when she was on holidays, a friend invited her to a party. It was an all-night dance party. A tall and dark-complexioned young man walked up to Ngozi for a dance, and she did not refuse.

This man was Mike. After the dance, Mike excused Ngozi for a talk outside. It was supposed to be a brief talk, but it turned out to be a very long one.

Mike introduced himself to Ngozi as an international businessman, while Ngozi said she was a final year student in the university.

"Ngozi, you see, we are just meeting for the first time but I want you to be the mother of all my children," Mike said to Ngozi.

"But I told you I'm still a student," Ngozi replied.

Mike told Ngozi that he was prepared to wait for her to complete her studies so they could settle down as husband and wife.

After that night, Ngozi and Mike started seeing each other regularly, but there were many things Mike never told Ngozi about himself and Ngozi was to regret later for hastily falling in love with him. Mike told Ngozi so many lies. To start with, Mike was the father of four children from four different girls. He never lived a settled life. He was always on the run from the police. All he wanted was to make Ngozi bear his fifth child.

There were times Ngozi would look for Mike but he was no where to be found. At such times, Mike and his gang of armed robbers would be somewhere robbing and killing and when he eventually surfaced he would tell Ngozi that there was an urgent call from his business partners abroad and he had to rush out of the country to attend to his business deals.

Mike and his gang had been arrested several times for vandalizing NEPA and NITEL property and each time they had always come out of the police station with smiling faces, because they had a boss who was a high ranking officer in the police force. It was through this unpatriotic police officer that all members of the gang got their fire arms.

Two men from Mike's gang were arrested at Onitsha as they tried to steal aluminium conductors from NEPA property, but Mike and others escaped. The arrested men later joined the gang, having been released through their normal connection.

In one of their operations, one of them was roasted alive by electricity as he tried to steal some cables. Immediately, he was electrocuted the rest of the gang melted away from the scene and they abandoned that line of operation. Ngozi was close to the truth one day when Mike and two members of the gang were arrested in an operation which was carried out along the Onitsha/Benin road. Two of the bandits met their waterloo as they were shot dead during a gun duel with the police.

Somebody who knew Mike saw him at the police station and the same person now passed on the information to Ngozi who now went to the station where she met Mike.

Later that day, Mike and the others were released once again. He lied to Ngozi that they were arrested for dangerous driving, and when they refused to bribe the policemen who arrested them, they were charged for armed robbery. Somehow Ngozi suspected that Mike was playing a fast one on her, but resolved not to question him further about his movements. One day, the truth would be revealed. It was only a matter of time. Mike passed the night in Ngozi's place and made love to her with greedy passion.

Eight

Every trader in Urhuoka went to Onitsha market, which was said to be the largest in Africa, to buy goods and this was where Dora also bought things from.

She had heard stories about the Onitsha road from motor accidents to robbery, so each time she had to travel, Dora would read her psalms and say her prayers before embarking on the journey.

Dora, having said her prayers to overcome all evil forces on the road on this particular day, she left for the motor park and where she boarded a vehicle to Onitsha. She was carrying a huge sum of money on her and just before the River Niger bridge, the car in which she and other traders were travelling was stopped by armed robbers.

All the traders including Dora were dispossessed of their money. The driver of the car who had wanted to mount some resistance was shot on the head and he died on the spot, one trader was shot on the leg while Dora and other women fled into a nearby bush as ordered by the robbers. A woman who had her right leg shot later bled to death. The two women that fled into the bush with Dora were so terrified that they walked into the bush without knowing where they were heading, but Dora stayed on her own in the bush near the road.

For a long time she was on her own and she did not know what the time was. She lost her neck chain and wrist watch to the bandits.

After the robbers had gone she walked down the road where she found the bodies of the driver and the woman in a pool of blood by the road side. None of the vehicles that passed by stopped to render help. While she was still thinking of what to do or where to go, a God-sent man came and who was Dora's saving grace. He was a handsome man. He was dressed in expensive guinea brocade with designer shoes. He looked rich from his dressing. When he came out of his yellow Mercedes Benz, he asked Dora if she was involved in a motor accident but Dora who was shivering said no and told him what had happened. The young man was full of pity for Dora and offered to help her.

The man, as Dora later got to know during their journey, was an international businessman. He gave his name as Victor Kagara. He was on his way to Onitsha too and he drove with Dora to Onitsha. At Onitsha, he took Dora to the market and bought her new clothes to change.

When she had changed to her new set of clothes, Victor gave her some money to go about her normal business and advised her to forget what had happened. Dora was so glad and thanked him several times.

While Victor was going down town to attend to the business that took him to Onitsha, Dora went to buy her goods from the market. In the evening she went to the place Victor and herself had agreed to meet. Victor was waiting when she got there. On their way home, he asked Dora many questions which she answered with all sincerity. At the end of the journey they had known much about each other. Victor was sympathetic towards Dora and promised to help her out of her dilemma.

Victor had lived in the United States since he was eight years old. He was taken to America by his uncle who was now late. Victor got his first degree when he was twenty. At the completion of his course, he went into business, dealing in second-hand cars and fridges, which he exported to his home country. Over the years, Victor had been able to put up three buildings, one for himself and the others for his aged parents.

He planned to marry at the age of twenty-five and he was just twenty-three when he met Dora. The girl he had wanted to marry was a Ghanaian but his parents kicked against this on tribal grounds. Since then he had not given marriage a second thought, until Dora came his way. He was from the same local government area with Dora and their villages were only separated by some bad roads. Now he made up his mind to settle down with Dora in the United States if only she would accept him as her husband.

Dora on her part was not in a hurry to marry, because to her, marriage should not be rushed into to avoid regrets at the end of the day. Two weeks after Victor gave Dora a lift along the busy Onitsha road, Victor travelled back to the United States and while he was there he was always thinking about Dora and they wrote to each other.

When he returned three months later, he decided to tell Dora his plans for her. He suggested that they should get married within two years. Dora agreed to this. Before Victor went back to America he took Dora to his parents and told them their plans. His parents were happy and Dora also took Victor to her only surviving Uncle, whom she got to know after the death of her father. She also took Victor to Ngozi's father. After the introduction, Victor left for the United States.

Nine

It was eight 0'clock on Friday evening and it was time for the local news on television. Hundreds of viewers in Urhuoka had already turned on their television sets to listen to the news. Ngozi was just getting home when the news started. The people of Urhuoka hardly miss the local news. Ngozi had a rough time getting to the house that evening, as a result of the heavy traffic congestion occasioned by fuel scarcity. The traffic was usually heavy at that time of the evening, when workers were returning home from their various places of work, but the situation had deteriorated since the fuel scarcity hit the nation because most vehicles had to queue for fuel and this would usually take-over most parts of the roads.

Ngozi was on time to catch up with the news, just as the newscaster began, "here is the news read by...." "first the headlines".

Five armed robbers were paraded on the television screen during the news. Of the five, two were already dead. The two were killed during a fierce gunfire exchange with the police. Mike was one of the three surviving robbers.

Ngozi could not believe what she saw on the screen. The truth had been revealed—It was Mike quite alright. He was wearing a pair of jeans, a black T-shirt and a pair of white canvass. That was exactly what he wore five days ago when Ngozi saw him last. He had told Ngozi that day he was going to Benin Republic on a business trip. Ngozi had insisted that he should put on more respectable clothes, instead of what he had on, but Mike who hardly listened to advice from women, refused.

Ngozi could not eat that night. The hunger she had felt earlier vanished. Tears freely flowed down her face. Ngozi buried herself in deep thought all through the night. Her suspicions about Mike had come to light.

The local newspapers had a field day the following morning as they filled their papers with the story of the spectacular robbery incident. The picture of Mike and his partners in crime were conspicuously placed in front of the newspapers with screaming headlines.

Dora had a copy of one of the newspapers. She was unable to listen to the news on television that night, as her area suffered a blackout. She rushed to Ngozi's place with the paper clutched in her hand, she found Ngozi crying and she soon joined in crying. For a long time the two friends cried freely.

Dora soon realized that crying was not going to help the situation, so she braced up and started comforting her dear friend.

"Take heart, Ngozi and stop crying, such is life. Do not weep so much over it". Dora said to her distressed friend. But Ngozi cried the more.

When Ngozi had finally stopped crying, Dora told her that she read about the ugly incident in the newspaper. She was afraid to show her the paper she was clutching as this could fuel the situation again.

"I have never one day trusted Mike because of his movement". Ngozi said in a calm voice.

"I know you have been complaining about him. It is good that the truth has come out and it is never too late to have a change of mind," Dora replied.

They talked for a very long time before Dora suggested that they should visit Mike at the police station.

¨But Dora, why do you think that I should leave this house to see that bastard Mike at the police station?" See him for what? I should see him because he has brought disgrace upon me? Over my dead body. I won't move an inch from this house."

"Ngozi, listen, visiting Mike does not mean anything serious," said Dora.

When Ngozi had taken her bath, she prepared lunch which both of them ate, after which they left for the police station where Mike was being held. Before they were allowed to see Mike, Dora gave the policemen one thousand naira, though she hated the police.

At the police station, Mike informed the two girls that he would appear in court before a judge on Monday with the other two robbers.

Ngozi rained insults on him when he asked her to come to the court on Monday. When the situation got out of hand, a police corporal supervising the visit, told the two friends to go home in their own interest.

On Monday when Ngozi reported for work she obtained permission to go to the hospital. She went to the tribunal instead, to listen to the case.

Fierce looking anti-crime policemen brought the robbers to court in a Black Maria and they were handcuffed. They were charged for robbing one Madam Kobi of x50,000 while armed with guns and other offensive weapons.

When the robbers pleaded not guilty to the charge, the armed robbery and firearms tribunal chairman ordered that the accused persons be remanded in prison custody.

Ngozi got back to the office later in the day, she was humiliated by her friends and she felt ashamed, but she never said a word to any of them.

When Dora visited her later that evening, Ngozi told her that Mike and his partners in crime had been remanded in prison custody. She also narrated how the girls in her office had behaved to her over the news they heard on television on that fateful Friday evening. But Dora advised her friend not to listen them.

〰〰〰〰〰〰〰〰〰〰〰〰〰〰〰〰〰

Ten

It was February 14th, Lagos was as busy as ever. At the Murtala Muhammed International Airport, some young men were discussing business deals, ranging from drug trafficking to oil bunkering.

At that moment, a plane arrived. The plane touched the tarmac at exactly 1.33p.m. and most people who were waiting anxiously for the arrival of the plane trooped out of the waiting hall to meet whoever they were expecting. Relations, friends and business partners exchanged pleasantries. But there was one young man, a Nigerian, who intentionally did not inform his people that he would be arriving Lagos on this day. He was Victor. As he beckoned to an airport taxi to take him to town, he was approached by a young man who asked if he had some dollars or pounds that he wanted to exchange into naira. Victor told him that he didn't require his services. Victor boarded a taxi to the motor park and off he left for his village. This was the first time Victor was travelling in this manner. In the past, he usually phoned his driver in advance to come to the airport to pick him up. This time he decided to pay a surprise visit. And he really took everybody by surprise when he arrived his village.

That afternoon, he drove in his yellow Mercedes Benz car to Dora's shop. Dora and a customer were discussing bribery and corruption, drug trafficking, advance fee fraud otherwise known as "419", oil bunkering and other forms of crime against the laws of the land that had become the order of the day, when all of a sudden Victor drove in slowly and parked in front of Dora's shop. They both embraced and kissed each other like starved lovers.

"But darling Victor, I was not expecting you," Dora said.

"Yes I know. I didn't inform anybody that I was coming because my middle name is "surprise", Victor replied Dora.

They talked for a very long time and at a point the customer took leave of them. That night after Dora had closed for the day, they both went out to various nite clubs the day being valentine's day. Both had a swell time. As they were driving out of the last hotel they visited, Dora remembered that she had left her purse behind and she asked Victor to stop so she could go for the purse. When Victor had packed the car properly along the road, Dora went back to the hotel, while Victor was waiting in the car. A moment later, a call girl walked up to Victor and said, "Hello my man, you are looking very clean this evening but it is like you're lonely. I could be your wife throughout the night if you don't mind. It is such a bad thing sitting there all alone. You know it's not good for men to sleep alone". Victor was rather surprised but managed to say something.

"Oh, thanks for the compliments. But if you would be my wife this night, who will then be my wife tomorrow?"

"Well, if you can pay my price of five thousand naira a night, no big deal, you could still take me as a wife if tomorrow comes", the girl told Victor.

"Sorry, I don't want an interim wife, look elsewhere for an interim husband tonight. I'm married, here comes my wife". At that moment Dora returned to the car. At the sight of the approaching Dora, the girl who could pass for a fourteen year old, lit a stick of cigarette she had taken out of her bag and vanished out of sight. Victor told Dora everything that transpired between him and the girl.

Dora, who had lived a very disciplined life, wondered why girls should turn themselves into

commodities. She was brought up in a disciplined home and she grew up to be the good girl her parents had always wanted her to be. Despite the fact that she lost her parents before she was nineteen, she
never thought of selling herself for money. Victor was her first love and they agreed to marry each other.

"Victor, but what do you think is the major reason why girls like this one behave the way they do?"

"You see, my pretty Dora, there are many reasons. Most of these girls are from poor homes, some of them are university graduates who could not secure jobs because of the unemployment problem in the country. Some of these girls are still in school but there is nobody to shoulder their responsibilities. They then choose to use what they have to get what they want. There is no social welfare scheme for citizens of this giant of Africa. Not everybody can stand the hardship in the country. We are living in a horrible world."

Throughout that night, Dora allowed the thought of that little girl to dominate her mind. She could have ended up that way if she hadn't been brought up in a disciplined home. Not even losing her parents when she needed them most made her to think of prostitution as a way to success in life. She believed that if Victor hadn't come into her life, she would have continued to struggle on her own, because she had the will to succeed.

Victor stayed for three weeks during which he was able to clear his goods at the port, before he returned to the United States.   On the day Victor left for the United

States, Dora insisted that she must see him off to the airport, so both of them travelled to Lagos and it was Dora's first visit to Lagos. She was fascinated with the beauty of Lagos. She pictured America in her mind and when she could not hold on to the thought any more she burst out suddenly.

"Darling Victor, tell me if Lagos could be so beautiful, how then would New York or London look like?"

"New York is a wonderful place my dear. Most of the houses there are sky-scrapers and you get things done easily there," Victor replied.

The ugly side of Lagos soon reared its head and this was the traffic problem. Although it was noon when they arrived Lagos with Victor's driver behind the wheel, every car moved at snail speed. When they got to Lagos, it took them an extra hour to get to the airport.

After lunch at the airport with Dora, Victor took the afternoon flight. Dora and the driver drove almost in silence back home, but Victor did promise Dora that he would write immediately he arrived the United States.

Night was falling when Dora and the driver got home.

〰〰〰〰〰〰〰〰〰〰〰〰〰

Eleven . . . .

Mike and the other robbers had stayed in prison custody for over six months. Dora and Ngozi were able to get a lawyer for him. The young lawyer told the two girls that in order to "dust" Mike's file lying in the office of the Director of Public Prosecutor (DPP) he would need x50,000.00. They were able to withdraw the amount from Mike's account and this was given to the lawyer. He promised that within a month the case would be tried and that the best he could do for Mike to escape execution was to change the robbery charge brought against him to stealing. According to him, with the money he could perform the miracle needed to change the armed robbery charge.

But the day the lawyer received the money was the last time he was seen by Ngozi, Dora and Mike. Nothing happened to the case file and Mike languished in detention with his friends, who never made any effort to get a lawyer.

One day when Dora and Ngozi visited Mike at the prison, they were asked to write an application for a visit by the warders they met. Having written it, the warders demanded fifty naira before they could be allowed to see him.

"Fine girls, no be the letter we go chop sha, una go bring one wazobia before una go see the man o", the warder who took the letter from Ngozi, stated in pidgin.

Dora pleaded with the warders that her father died as a retired assistant superintendent of prisons. The warders refused saying that has been the system and that her late father was in the system before he retired. The warders were given the amount they demanded, then one of them who wore a faded and half torn uniform languidly walked to the cell with a bunch of keys and brought Mike to the visitor's room.

Mike narrated the brutal and horrible conditions of the prison to the two girls. He said they slept in shifts on a filthy and smelly bare floor and this had affected his skin, and at the same time his health was failing.

"We're about one hundred and thirty inmates in one cell meant for thirty inmates," Mike told the girls as he responded aggressively to the itching of his body.

Ngozi continued to visit Mike in prison and on each occasion Mike complained about the horrible food in prison. He described life in prison as brutal, nasty and filthy. He thought he could survive it. On one of her visits, Ngozi brought Mike a piece of sad news. Mike's father was attacked and killed by a gang of five armed robbers.

It was alleged, that Mike's father was a supplier of locally made pistols and charms for armed bandits. Apparently, the charms he prepared for the gang failed and two of the gang men were killed in a crossfire with the police. When they returned to Mike's father, he thought they came for the usual supply of arms and charms, but they told him their mission was to eliminate him.

"Now, say your last prayers as you must die as our friends died," one of the die-hard armed robbers said to Mike's father and at that moment one of the robbers shot him in the head. It was pain, blood and death on the spot.

Mike wept like a baby when Ngozi had finished narrating how his father's life ended. By this time, he had spent two years in detention without trial.

At this time, when Mike's father was killed by the robbers, the gang went into war with the police for killing the leader of the gang.

One night when the robbers were out for the police at a busy junction, they met two policemen extorting money from motorists and they opened fire on them. They removed the uniforms of the dead policemen and went away with them. During this period too, some policemen dressed in mufti when going to work. It was a reign of terror, and the police lost to the underworld men.

Six months after the death of Mike's father, a can of worms was opened. Victor in far away America got a clue of the death of Joe. From investigations carried out by a committee of friends it was revealed that Mike was among the three men that picked up Joe from the airport and took him to their boss, Badmiller. It was three of them that also took the body of Joe to Urhuoka.

Victor got this information across to Dora fast through a letter and assured her that although there was no clue yet on the whereabouts of Badmiller, no effort would be spared to track him down to face the music.

"And more importantly Dora, we got information here recently through a reliable source that two of the bastards were killed by policemen and as for Mike there is little or nothing that can be done about him, since he is now in detention for a robbery charge."

Dora later passed on the information to Ngozi and the two girls regretted ever assisting him.

"I'm very sorry about the involvement of that devil called Mike in Joe's death. Wish we had known earlier about this," said Ngozi.

"Well life is like that. We never knew Mike was connected with the death of my brother thereby putting me into much suffering," Dora said as she burst into tears.

She was comforted by Ngozi who made up her mind never to visit Mike again in detention. Mike died in custody, but before he died he had sent prison warders several times to Ngozi but she refused to see him again.

Twelve . . .

Dora's business was becoming more demanding of her time. There were times when she had to close her shop for days to travel to Onitsha or Cotonou in Benin Republic.

On one of such trips to Onitsha, she meet a young lady in the taxi they were travelling in and they became friends instantly. When Dora complained about how she usually had to close her shop when she had to travel, the young lady advised her to employ a sales girl who would run the place for her when she was away.

"I have tried to look for one, but getting a good sales girl seems an uphill task," Dora had told the lady.

"In that case I'll look out for one for you," the lady said.

The next morning, the young lady brought a girl, Meg, who was a year older than Dora, to be her sales girl. Dora was very pleased at this but she nursed some fear as to whether the girl could be trusted.

Dora agreed to put Meg on probation. She employed her and they agreed on a monthly salary of one thousand and fifty naira.

Dora also engaged the services of tailors who made men and women's clothes which she took to Cotonou and in return she brought back bales of second hand clothes to sell. She occasionally sold off the clothes in Lagos before arriving Urhuoka. No doubt, Dora had become a successful business woman.

Meg had been job hunting for over two years after finishing secondary school. She had tried to secure a job as a secretary/typist but without success. She attended so many interviews but she was always told, "you will hear from us" and she never got any feedback from them.

"I cannot understand the problem with this country. Everyday, there are adverts in the newspapers. One would apply and be invited for interview but one never gets the job." That was exactly what she said to a friend a some time ago, after another disappointment.

What Meg never knew was that, she failed to "see" the people in power in those companies. It did not matter whether you had all the qualifications in the world, what mattered was who you knew and how tight your connections were.

Corruption had become the problem in our society and this was what Dora and Meg discussed one day in the shop. A very cordial relationship existed between Dora and Meg. They talked freely and one could hardly know who was the employer or the employee.

"Meg getting a job or admission in school depends on who you know and not what you know," Dora stated.

"It is a rotten society, my sister. What about the law enforcement agents on our roads who have turned beggars, instead of doing the work which they are paid to do," Meg chipped in.

"Corruption starts from the top, those uniformed men usually make returns to those at the top. The system must be overhauled starting from the top," Dora added.

"But come to think of it, who do you think will overhaul the rotten system?" A flabbergasted Meg, who had been a victim of the system, asked.

After another unsuccessful interview, Meg vowed never to attend any other. It was during this period when she was at home doing nothing that her neighbour brought her to Dora and luckily enough she was offered the job. Although the salary was nothing to write home about, she accepted it because half a loaf, they say, is better than none.

Their interactions brought them very close to each other. Meg proved to be a faithful and hard working girl. Dora compensated her for her dedication to duty.

One day, Meg told Dora about her friend, Philo. They had been classmates. Philo and Meg tried to secure jobs after leaving school but to no avail.

According to Meg, Philo tried her hands on virtually everything, one after the other. She tried hair dressing for three months and abandoned it for fashion designing, which she also abandoned after four months. Philo had so many lovers and she had many abortions. She was used by men and dumped like a wet blanket at the end of the day.

"Meg, there is nothing as good as discovering one's self and knowing exactly   where one fits into in our decayed society."

"It is true one should make up one's mind on what to become and pursue that goal to the end," said Meg.

Meg told Dora that the society was frustrating. As she was talking, a customer walked in and she attended to her.

When the customer had gone, the two girls started their discussion again; they blamed the woes of the society on the leaders who were ready to do anything to perpetuate themselves in office at the expense of the people.

"I hate hearing our leaders talk about discipline when they are not disciplined themselves. Some of them cannot even manage their homes yet they want to rule you and me," Dora stated.

"And you see," Dora said again, "our nation has become a funny place. The number one seat has become an all-comers' ambition. Even those that cannot control their wives and children at home want to occupy it because they have the guns and the wealth. And they are ready to tell the whole world that: *We don't know those who will succeed us, but we know those who will not succeed us.* They are ready to do anything to frustrate the ambitions of those whose faces they hate to see. What we have today is the government of the corrupt, by the corrupt, and for the corrupt. *Oh My beloved country, I hail thee.*"

"A corrupt leader is not a disciplined leader. If the leader is corrupt there is the tendency for the followers to be corrupt, at the end of the day we have a group of indisciplined leaders controlling the affairs of our dear fatherland. We don't have honest leaders and that is the bane of the society," Dora said.

"Yes and that reminds me of what one of my teachers said a long time ago," said Meg.

"What did he say?" Dora asked.

He said " . . . the good child is the one that obeys his parents and elders, and never does wrong". He said also, " . . . for a child to be disciplined so as to become a good product of the society, such a child must have the fear of God at heart and the parents must be very disciplined too."

"But Meg, how many of us today still have the fear of God in our hearts when even the pastors are guilty?"

"That reminds me of the story of Philo, which I have not concluded," Meg stated.

According to Meg, Philo had gone out with all the men in town and age was fast telling on her. She started attending a spiritual church, praying for a husband but no one came her way.

One day, Philo met one Alhaji who was new in town, and they quickly fell in love. Three months after the relationship started, Philo started making excuses each time Alhaji asked her out. She had joined one of the numerous Pentecostal churches and became a "born again".

"She started preaching to the Alhaji, asking him to repent of all his sins. Philo succeeded in taking Alhaji to her church one day and the Alhaji was introduced to the pastor of the church. Philo was also fond of preaching to young girls too about the dangers of knowing a man before marriage, but as she was doing this her mind was far away from what she preached. She was not truly a born again as she claimed to be.

"Nemesis caught up with her one day when Alhaji saw her in a hotel with another man.

"Alhaji had on the previous day arranged that they should spend a night together, but she refused saying she would be attending an all night prayer meeting in the church.

"Alhaji who didn't want to be a stumbling block allowed her to have her way. That was the night she was supposed to be in the church. Alhaji found solace in another girl, who offered to spend the night with him provided he could pay her price of one thousand and five hundred naira. Alhaji was surprised when he found Philo with another man in the same hotel where he had gone to spend the night.

Meg continued as Dora listened attentively. "Ironically, the man Philo was found with was no other than the pastor of the church."

"Wonders shall never end", Dora shouted.

It was a funny coincidence. It happened that Alhaji and the girl were in the bar and took their seats at the far end of the bar, which was a bit dark.

"The glass of beer Alhaji was holding dropped onto the floor". At first he was in doubt whether that was Philo but her figure and even the face of the pastor whom he had met while attending the church on Philo's invitation were not a mistaken identity.

"When Philo and her pastor had finished drinking, they went upstairs to the room they had booked for the night", Meg added. "They were regular customers in the hotel, so their apartment was always reserved for them.

"As they were climbing the staircase, Alhaji once again had a clear view of them. It was Philo and her pastor, alright.

"The room Alhaji booked for the night was opposite the one Philo and her pastor occupied. In the morning of the following day, as Philo and her pastor were checking out, Alhaji who was already awake, opened his door with only a pair of pyjamas on and met face to face with Philo and her pastor and greeted them, "Oh, Philo good morning, man of God how was your night?" Both

Philo and the pastor were speechless. They wished the ground would open and swallow them.

"Alhaji quickly saved the situation by withdrawing into his hotel apartment. After a little while, he heard footsteps along the passage until they faded away. It was only five-fifteen in the morning. Philo and the pastor were in a hurry to leave the hotel premises, to avoid people noticing a man of God and a "born-again sister" checking out of a hotel apartment. That was the last Alhaji ever saw of Philo.

"So, Dora, when Philo could not see her menses, she told the Pastor about it and his eyes became red like fire, as he was very annoyed. He gave her money to remove "the devil's seed".

"The pastor said, *you must remove that devil's seed from your womb, lest you bring disgrace to me and ruin my lucrative church business.*

"When Philo had seen the doctor and the *devil's seed* was removed, she never went back to the church. Up till now nobody can ascertain her whereabouts," Meg concluded.

"Meg, the pastor must have treated other self acclaimed born-again sisters like that."

"Well that is a man of God for you," Meg said.

~~~~~~~~~~~~~~~~~~~~~~~~~~~~~~~~

Thirteen
~~~~~~~~~~~~~~~~~~~~~~~~~~~~~~~~

Dora travelled on a business trip to the Republic of Benin when Victor arrived from the United States. It had been exactly nine months since he left for America. He had always been in constant touch with Dora.

Dora on her part, was aware that Victor would be in town very soon, so she decided to make the last trip to the Republic of Benin before his arrival.

It was arranged that their wedding would take place when Victor came to town, and both of them were expected to leave for the United States immediately after the wedding.

On this particular trip, Dora did not return as planned and Meg became very worried, so also was Victor, because two days had passed since his arrival and there was no news from Dora yet.

"Oga, Madam nor dey stay long like dis before," Meg told Victor, who called at Dora's shop that afternoon.

He assured Meg that if Dora failed to return that day, he would have no choice but to go and look for her the following day in the Republic of Benin.

Meanwhile, Dora had been in detention for being in possession of contraband goods. She was arrested on her way back by the customs men of that country just before the car in which she was travelling got to the last border post.

Normally, Dora and her co-travellers would not have spent a night in the customs cell at the border posts had they "settled" the men who arrested them. Dora was willing to pay her share but others were not co-operative.

Victor was saved from travelling the next day to search for her because the other traders later spoke in unison on the need to pay the "settlement" and leave the customs net. All the traders were in possession of foreign wine and several bags of imported rice. Dora purchased these items in view of her traditional marriage and the church wedding.

The Nigerian customs officials also arrested the traders on arrival in Nigeria but the traders quickly "settled" them.

Meg was about to close for the day when Dora arrived that evening and not quite long after her arrival, a worried Victor came to the shop. Dora narrated her ordeal to them. When she had finished telling the story, Victor drove her to her house and Meg was dropped off at a particular point, where she could find her way home.

Dora could not go to the shop the following day, because she needed all the rest in the world, having spent sleepless nights in the customs cell at the border post. That evening, Meg came to the house to render her accounts to Dora for the days she was away. Dora was impressed with the sales Meg made in her absence.

As a result of the marriage preparations, Victor Kagara and Dora Zome were very busy. Victor was always in constant touch with Dora's uncle and other members of her family.

Dora's absence was always noticed at her shop. In the evening of the second month after Victor had arrived for the marriage, the traditional marriage ceremony took place with friends, relations and well wishers in attendance. Dora almost turned that moment of joy in her life into sadness as she cried openly.

Dora was crying because her parents were not alive to witness her marriage. She had seen how mothers were honoured on the day of their daughter's marriage but on the day of her own marriage, no mother, no father, no sister and not even a brother was there and she felt very sad.

Before the ceremony kicked off she had called herself to order and accepted what death denied her. The women who came to the marriage and several of her friends advised her to forget about what had happened and concentrate on the present. One of the women told Dora a pathetic story of a young girl who lost her mother in a ghastly motor accident a day before her wedding.

"My daughter, although the marriage was postponed for sometime, but it still took place, not too long after the burial. In your case, try to put the memory of your parents behind you and do not spoil your day," one of the women advised Dora.

Ngozi also helped Dora to put her mind at ease. "Dora, it is hard to forget those sad moments that are weighing down on you. Today is your day, a woman has but one day like this to cherish. Remember too that we are all born to live and to die but what we don't know is how and when," Ngozi said to her childhood friend.

When Dora had listened to all the advice, she no longer allowed the thoughts of her late parents to disturb her mind as she braced up to make the day a memorable one in her life.

The wedding ceremony could be best described as a festival. It attracted people from far and wide. There was enough food and drink for everybody. Those who were not present that day came for their share the following day and were dumbfounded to see food and drinks still flowing. Some people went home with bowls of pounded yam, eba, fried rice, meat and soup.

Payment of the bride price took place inside Dora's father's house. Traditional dance troupes and local musicians entertained the crowd. The women groups were given bags of salt while the men got several containers of local gin. The celebrants constantly rained hard currency on the dancers and others .

People who witnessed the ceremony were of the view that they had never before seen such a grand traditional wedding event. The young girls around envied Dora for being a lucky girl. Many had forgotten how sad life had been to Dora in the past.

Seven days after the traditional marriage, the church wedding took place. Those who missed the first ceremony were the first to arrive at the wedding reception.

Canopies were erected everywhere and the surrounding roads were closed. Victor and Dora were in high spirits. They were carried away by the calibre of people present in the church as the wedding drew the cream of the society.

As a result of the huge turnout the couple only heard half of the pastor's preaching. The pastor while quoting from the Book of Mark, said, "for this reason a man shall leave his father and mother and be joined to his wife, and the two shall become one flesh. So they are no longer two but one flesh. What therefore God has joined together, let no man put asunder."

But because Victor's mind was far away from what the pastor was saying, he made to kiss Dora on her lips at the last word of the Pastor and the whole congregation burst into laughter. Victor realised that it was not yet time for that aspect of the ceremony.

Before the wedding, Dora had asked her dedicated salesgirl Meg, and good friend Ngozi, to inherit her business.

The following day, Victor and Dora now legally married left for America to begin a new life.

<hr>

Fourteen

Little Agatha was only four years old, when she became seriously ill. Her parents took her to various hospitals for cure without much success. The little girl made the parents panic. At a time she was admitted into a nearby government owned hospital, but there is this peculiar "out-of stock problem" in government hospitals: Drugs are not always available in government hospitals. They usually find their way into private clinics owned by doctors who work in government hospitals. Agatha spent over a week in the hospital and there were no drugs for her. Her parents bought the drugs doctors administered on her throughout the period from a drugs store just outside the hospital gate. When the parents were fed up with the western method of treatment they asked that Agatha be discharged and she was taken to a spiritual church, where the parents were asked to fast for seven days for her. Having spent fourteen days in the church with seven days of intensive fasting and prayers, Agatha's case worsened and the parents were on the march again to save her life. For every night Agatha stayed in the church, the prophet made her parents to buy three packets of candles from his wife who dealt in candles and other spiritual items. The candles were in different colours of white, black and red.

When her condition did not improve she was taken to a renowned witch doctor who revealed many things to the parents. He told them that when Agatha was grown up and ready for marriage, no bride price should be paid on her, because Agatha will die on the day the money was collected from the prospective bride-groom. The native doctor said when Agatha first came to the world, she died during a fight with the husband. As a result of what was still sleeping when they got there. The parents, were glad to see their child again.

Agatha became well after and when the parents got home they informed no one about the warning of the native doctor that no bride price should be paid on her when she was grown and ready for marriage. Not even their two grown up children were informed.

Many years later, when she went on holidays to her uncle's place far away from their village, fire razed down her parents house one night and her elder brother, sister, mother and father were burnt to death in the inferno. Thereafter, she lived with the uncle in Ukwandia.

One Sunday afternoon when Agatha and others had returned from church, a young man whom Agatha introduced to his uncle as Paul Zome came to see her. Agatha told the uncle, when Paul had gone, that both of them were in love.

When Agatha finished her Secondary School, the uncle gave her to Paul Zome in marriage. The uncle, unaware of the warning that no bride price should be paid on Agatha, summoned members of the family together and, in a colourful ceremony, her bride price was paid. That night, Agatha collapsed and died. After the burial, the young man fled out of Ukwandia because he was badly shaken by the incident.

Before Paul became a wealthy young man, he had gained admission into one of the nation's universities but during his third year, he and four other undergraduates were expelled because of their involvement in secret cult happened to her in her first life she wouldn't want a bride price to be paid on her in her second life. Moreover, she had a husband she was keeping in the spirit world. When the native doctor had finished consulting with the oracle he advised the parents to carry out some sacrifices.

In the middle of the night, Agatha was placed inside a big calabash and was carried on the head by the errand boy of the native doctor. The native doctor led the way, accompanied by the father and distressed mother. When they had gone very far from the village, they got to a junction where three roads met in a thick bush. Here the sacrifice was carried out. The native doctor spread a white piece of cloth on the ground and a white cock was slaughtered. The blood was sprinkled on the white cloth. The native doctor made tiny cuts on Agatha's body with a very sharp razor before laying her on the white cloth. Agatha started crying as a result of the pain from the cuts. Her cry echoed far into the dark night, she was still crying when the native doctor threw mashed yam mixed with palm oil around her.

Having recited several incantations, the witch doctor told her parents that Agatha will pass the night in the bush alone. The parents were very worried, especially the mother, who started to cry but the native doctor assured them that no harm would come upon Agatha.

Before they left the scene of the sacrifice, the native doctor covered Agatha with a piece of red cloth. In the morning, the native doctor and his errand boy went to the spot of the sacrifice to fetch Agatha for her parents. She activities in the campus. After he was sent out of the university, his mother, Clara who was a petty trader felt unhappy because since she packed it up with Paul's father, she had borne all the responsibilities of caring for the three children she had from the marriage.

To add to her problem after Paul had been expelled from the university, her business centre along the road was demolished by the state environmental task force. The demolition of the illegal structures affected many people. Paul's mother was able to raise some money from members of her club with which Paul started a spare parts business.

At the age of thirty Paul, had made his first million naira. He got a store for his mother in the market where she dealt in women's and babies clothes.

Paul saw Agatha's death on the day of their traditional marriage as a bad omen. Three years after, Paul met Ngozi. When Dora and Victor left for America, Ngozi felt sad for a while as she missed her friend and it was during this period that she met Paul.

Before Ngozi fled her place, she had asked Meg for her own share of the proceeds of their business.

It was on their third meeting that Ngozi got to know that Paul was Dora's half brother and Paul was glad to know that Ngozi and his sister Dora were good friends.

That night, Ngozi told Paul how their father died some hours before he was to be discharged from the hospital and the problem she waded through with Dora when the old man fell ill, how Dora struggled on her own after the death of their father before she got married to Victor, but never mentioned Mike's involvement in Joe's death.

Paul also told Ngozi how he had tried to trace his father and other members of the family without success. Paul told Ngozi about Agatha too.

The following day, Ngozi and Paul tried to get Dora on the telephone but they could not get through. They eventually got through after several days of trying. Dora had just returned from evening lectures when the telephone rang. She was so glad about the great discovery.

During the telephone conversation, Dora informed Ngozi and Paul that she had gained admission into one of the best universities in the United States to study Mass Communication, her dream course.

Paul wanted to speak with his in-law, Victor, but was informed by   Dora that he was out attending a conference.

"Oh, my big brother Paul, it was the last prayer of our father before he rested with his ancestors that we should find each other. I'm glad that his prayer has been answered."

"Dora, I've been so worried about the situation. You see, the world is a small place, I'm so happy too that we found each other. It's just a matter of time, we must surely see face to face one of these days," Paul said.

"Please Paul, treat my friend Ngozi nicely because she is a very good girl. She and her father really assisted me. I will not forget them.

"Yes, she told me everything. Maybe it's a way of compensating her that God has brought the two of us together. God has a way of doing things, you know. We were separated in the past, then we found each other and now your best friend, Ngozi, is all that I live for in this world. She is itching to speak with you, please tell Victor that I will write him immediately."

"That is nice of you, I'll pass on your message, bye. Let's have Ngozi on the line". Paul handed the telephone to Ngozi and they talked for a long time without minding the cost of the call.

After that first conversation, Dora and Paul were in constant touch with each other but when the wedding between Paul and Ngozi took place, Dora and Victor could not honour their invitation. To compensate them, Victor had sent Paul and Ngozi a round trip ticket for their honeymoon in United States.

A night before their departure, Paul and Ngozi phoned Victor and Dora to receive them at the airport.

THE END

We are in a society where everyone is for himself and God for all. No wonder after the death of Dora's father and brother, there was nobody to send her to the university, but with self determination, she realized her dreams . . .

Corruption has eaten deep into the fabric of our society. Public office holders are worshipped for looting the nation.

Government hospitals have become mere consulting clinics. Law enforcement agents take bribes and look the other way.

Employment for the army of the unemployed is now a mirage - as jobs for all has been reserved till the year 2000. No wonder our young men are forced into drugs and violent crimes.

What do you think could be left of a society where a Pastor of a church could impregnate one of the "born-again sisters" and even sponsor the abortion? Practically nothing but a rotten and smelling society.

The author, Mr. Dennis Otu, studied Journalism. He worked for the following newspapers;

THE OBSERVER, THE WATCHMAN, DELTA WEEKLY. At a time he was made the judicial correspondent of WEEKEND COURIER.

He is a memebr of the Nigeria Union of Journalists (NUJ) and an Associate member Association of Nigerian Authors.

He is, at present a reporter with the Delta State Government owned newspaper – THE POINTER.

He is the author of QUOTES OF WHO'S WHO and LOVE MADE EASY.